W9-ACR-291

Sneakers, the Seaside Cat

by Margaret Wise Brown
illustrated by Anne Mortimer

HarperCollins*Publishers*

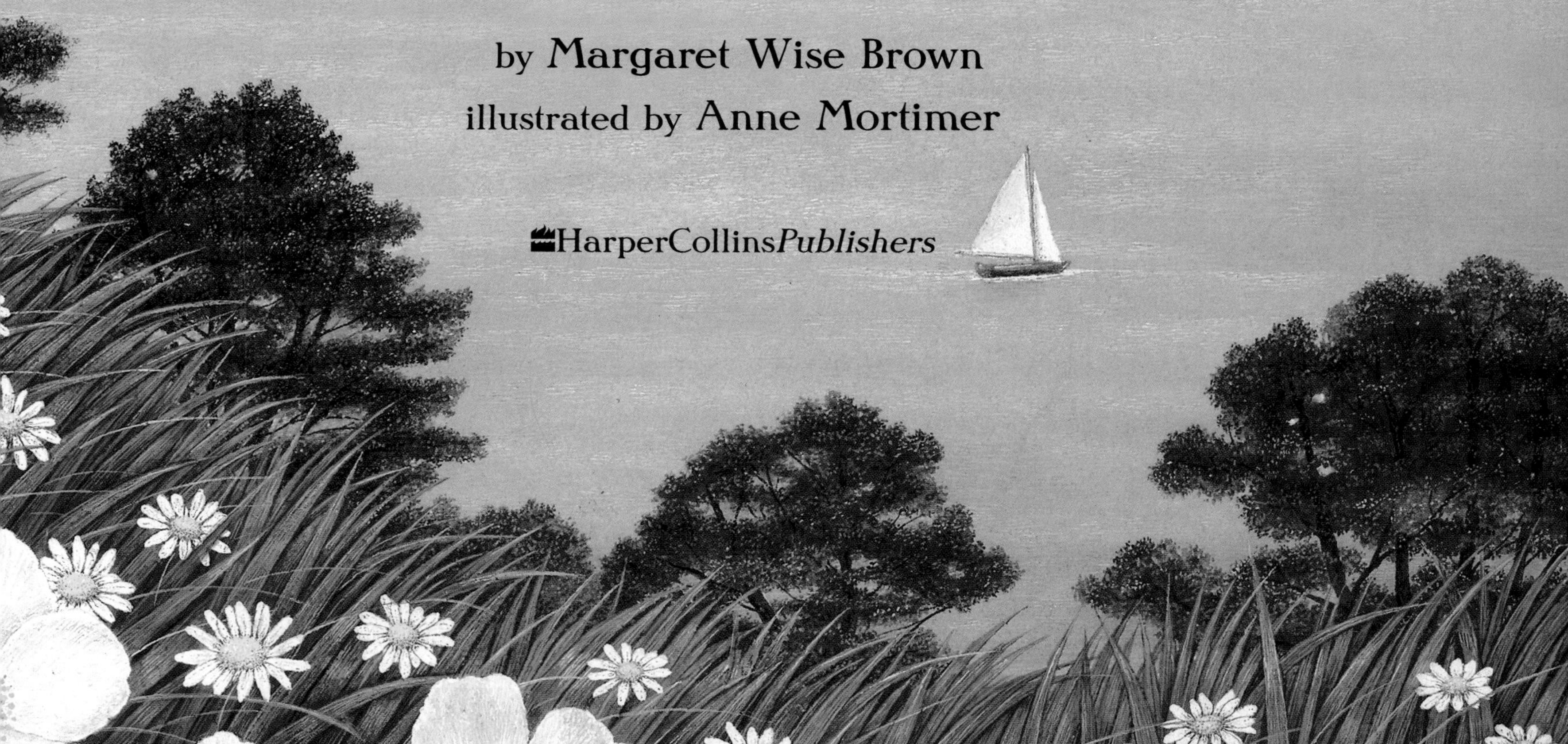

Sneakers, the Seaside Cat

www.harperchildrens.com

Library of Congress Cataloging-in-Publication Data
Brown, Margaret Wise, date.
Sneakers, the seaside cat / by Margaret Wise Brown ; illustrated by Anne Mortimer.
p. cm.
Summary: Sneakers the cat visits the sea for the first time, where he chases butterflies, listens to seashells, and plays with crabs.
ISBN 0-06-028692-X — ISBN 0-06-028693-8 (lib. bdg.)
[1. Cats—Fiction. 2. Beaches—Fiction. 3. Ocean—Fiction.] I. Mortimer, Anne, ill. II. Title.
PZ7.B8163 Sm 2003
[E]—dc21 2002024235

Typography by Elynn Cohen 1 2 3 4 5 6 7 8 9 10 ❖ First Edition

To Emma and Charlie

—A.M.

Once there was a little fat cat, and his name was Sneakers. He had four white paws and almost all the rest of him was inky black. He lived with a little boy and his father and his mother.

One day the little boy and his father and his mother went to the seashore.

When Sneakers came to the sea, he was delighted.

He could smell the fish. He thought he could catch them like mice.

But when he dipped his careful little white paw into the blue sea, the water was wet. And it was cold. So Sneakers decided to go out in a field and look for mice instead.

The field was full of butterflies, so Sneakers chased one. But the sea was bothering him. All around him he could smell it, beyond the smell of the pine trees. And he could feel it. It excited him. And way off he could still hear it.

Boom! Boom! Boom!

Sneakers did not know that *boom, boom, boom* was the sea pounding the rocks way off shore, out on the ledges of the sea.

Then he heard *Ha-ha-ha! Scree! Scree!*
He wondered what it was.

First it was
a shadow. Then
it was a bird. Only it
was such a big bird
it didn't seem very
frightened of a little black
cat with white paws. Sneakers
didn't like to think about birds
who are not afraid of cats, so he
went for a walk on the beach.

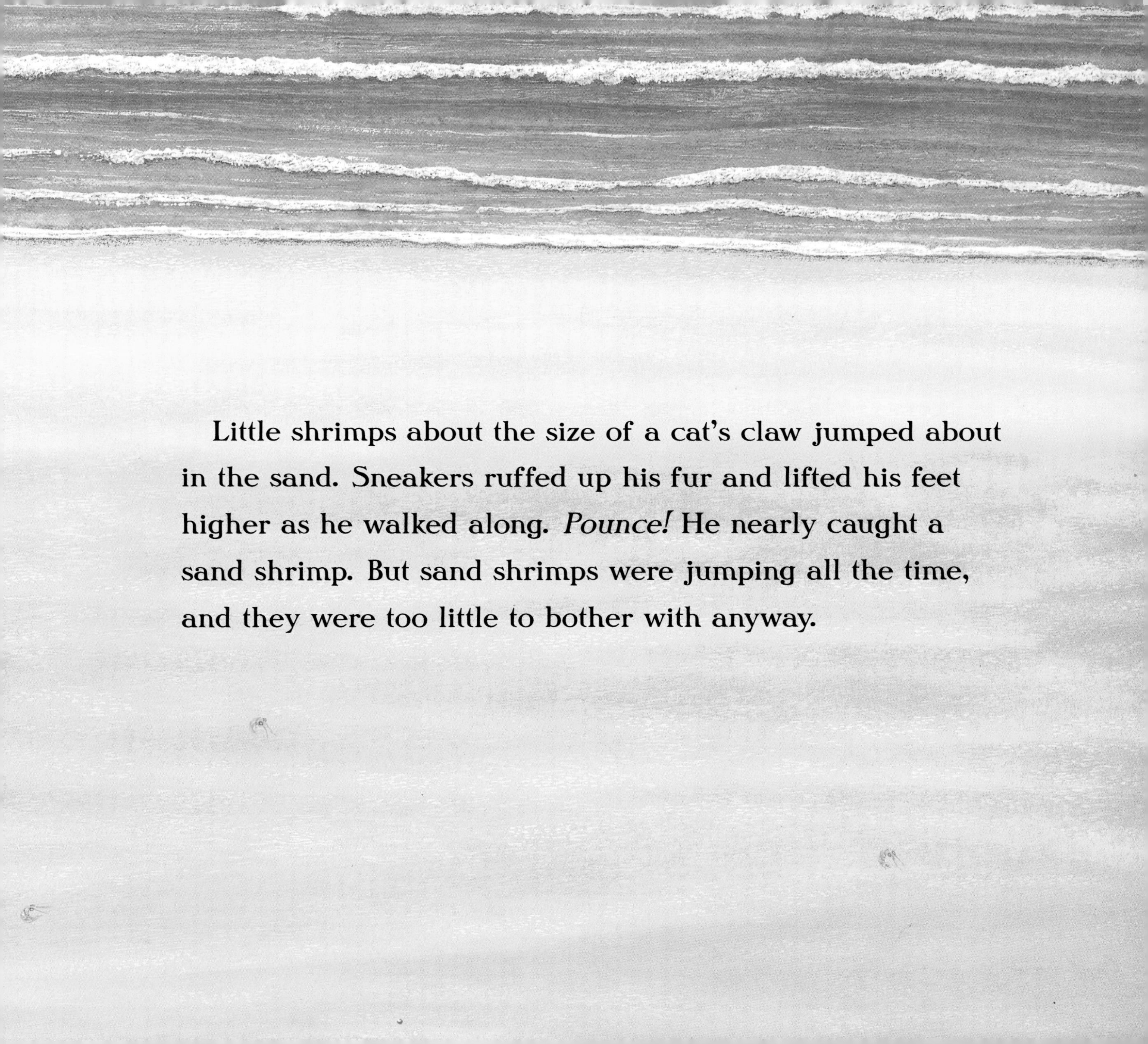

Little shrimps about the size of a cat's claw jumped about in the sand. Sneakers ruffed up his fur and lifted his feet higher as he walked along. *Pounce!* He nearly caught a sand shrimp. But sand shrimps were jumping all the time, and they were too little to bother with anyway.

Then up ahead, on the yellow sand, Sneakers saw something. It was yellow and pink on the outside. Sneakers had never seen anything that shape before. Then he crept up to it and peeked in. There was nothing in it. He put his head down to it and listened. There was a roar like the ocean's roar in it. But there was nothing in the shell. So he lifted up his paws and he walked along the beach some more.

He saw a big flat thing with long bent legs. Sneakers could see the two black shiny eyes sticking out of its head. Sneakers crept after it. But the crab's eyes stuck so far out of its head that they had seen Sneakers coming. The crab scuttled down to the water's edge. But Sneakers was too quick for it. He hit the crab with his paw to see what it would do.

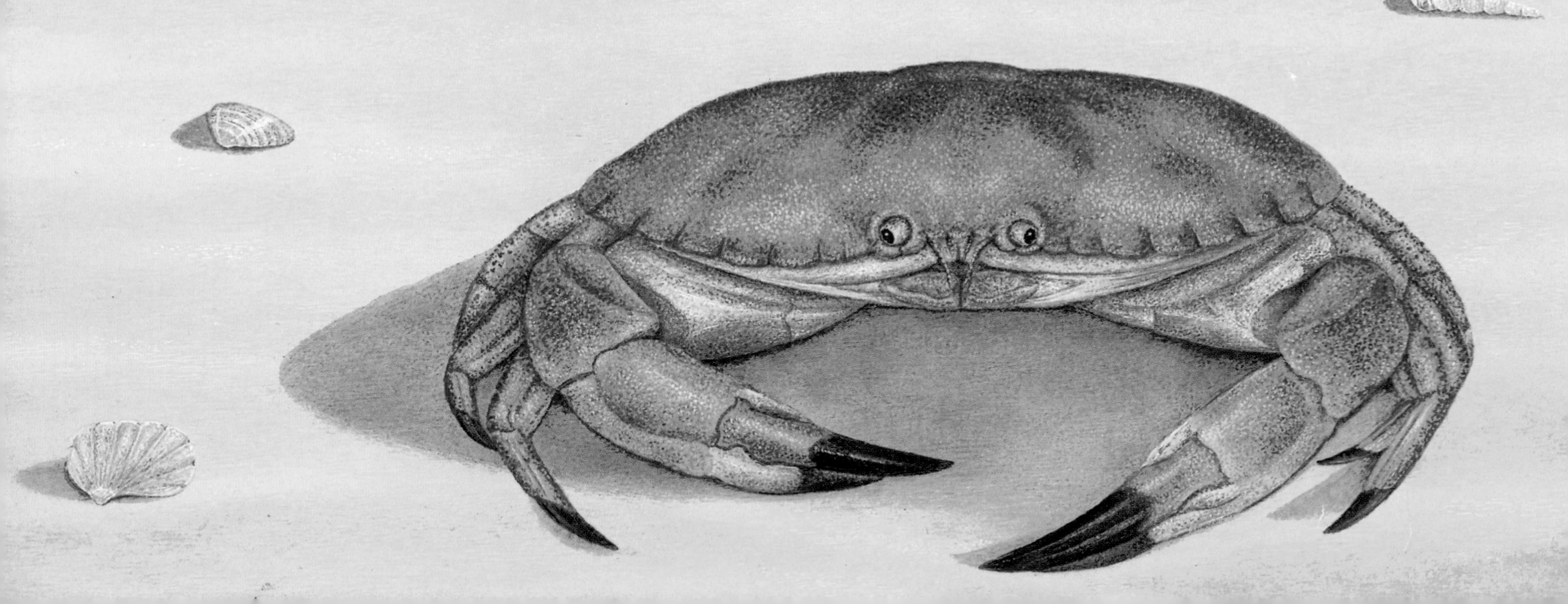

And this is what the crab did.

The crab shot out one of its long bent legs and grabbed ahold of Sneakers' little white paw in its crab claw. It hung on and pinched Sneakers a little. Sneakers didn't like that at all. He snatched his paw back so fast that the crab fell off. Then he licked his paw and ruffed out his fur and walked on down the beach.

Something was happening in the air. The air was wetter and heavier. Sneakers could feel it on his tender little nose. And when he looked around there were great puffs of smoke blowing in from the sea. They smelled of the sea and came drifting in, in puffs as big as clouds, until you couldn't see the sun anymore. Everything was gray and the land beyond was all dim and dark like one big shape.

"My, but I'm glad I saw that," thought Sneakers.

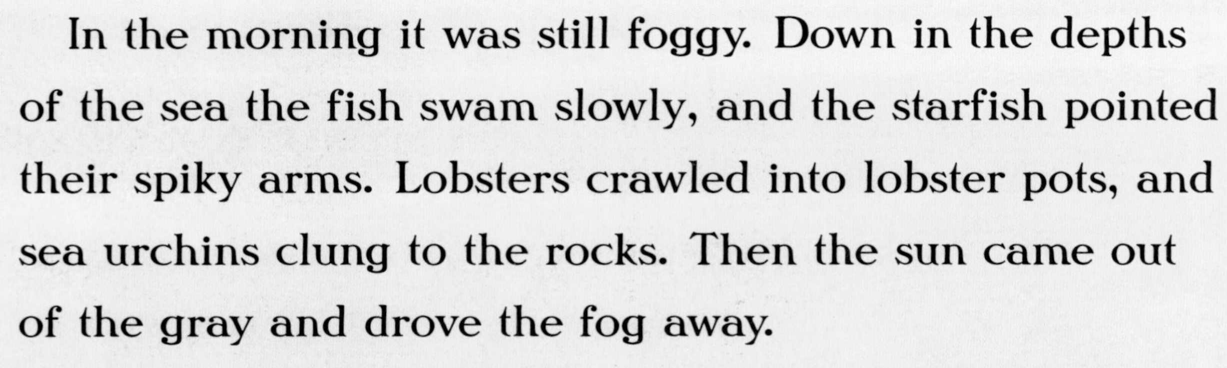

In the morning it was still foggy. Down in the depths of the sea the fish swam slowly, and the starfish pointed their spiky arms. Lobsters crawled into lobster pots, and sea urchins clung to the rocks. Then the sun came out of the gray and drove the fog away.

It was low tide and all around was seaweed. Then Sneakers heard a little sound. It was like creaky breathing. It was the seaweed popping. "My, I'm glad I heard that," said Sneakers.

And he sat and warmed himself in the sunlight and watched the light on the waves.

The next day, Sneakers and his family left the seashore. All the way home in the car Sneakers thought soft little cat thoughts about the sea.

Deep in the fog a sea-slung gong
sleepily rocks to its
ding, dong, dong.

Hark to the sound
of the sea-slung gong,
ding, dong, dong,
ding, dong, dong.